What lies at the end of the rainbow? Is there merely a pot of gold, or might there be another sort of treasure — a treasure that may be reached by anyone willing to undertake the journey?

For if you follow the rainbow to its end and look into its shimmering colors, you will find a great oak tree with a door at the base of the trunk.

If you open the door and step inside, you will meet Mrs. Murgatroyd™, the wise woman who lives there. In her paint pots she collects all the colors of the rainbow.

And if you take up a paintbrush and picture whatever is in your heart, you will discover a treasure far more valuable than gold.

Nightmares in the Mist

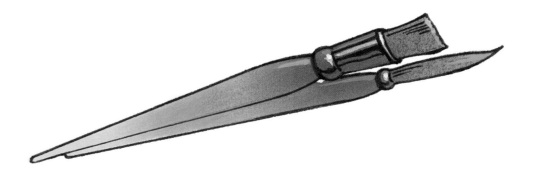

Series concept by Ayman Sawaf and Kevin Ryerson
Developed from actual case histories by art therapist Liz Farrington
Copyright ©1994 by Enchanté Publishing
MRS. MURGATROYD character copyright ©1993 by Enchanté
MRS. MURGATROYD is a trademark of Enchanté
Series format and design by Jaclyne Scardova
Edited by Gudrun Höy. Story editing by Bobi Martin

Enchanté Publishing
P.O. Box 620471, Woodside, CA 94062

Printed in Singapore

Library of Congress Cataloging-in-Publication Data
Farrington, Liz.
Nightmares in the mist/story created by Liz Farrington; written by Leslie McGuire;
illustrated by Brian McGovern. — 2nd ed.
          p.   cm.
Summary: With the help of Mrs. Murgatroyd's magical paints, Alicia overcomes the
fears that have bothered her since her mother went into the hospital.
ISBN 1-56844-103-7
[1. Fear - Fiction. 2. Parent and child - Fiction] I. McGuire, Leslie.
II. McGovern Brian, ill. III. Title.
PZ7.F24618N1   1995   (Fic.)—dc20   95-36445

Second Edition
10 9 8 7 6 5 4 3 2 1

Nightmares in the Mist

Story created by Liz Farrington
Written by Leslie McGuire
Illustrated by Brian McGovern

Enchanté Publishing

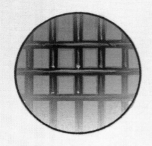

It was after her again! Alicia felt surrounded by a thick mist. The roaring, clanking noise got louder and louder. Now she could see the monster's glaring red eye. She tried to get away but something grabbed her arm! She opened her mouth to scream but no sound came out.

"Alicia," said her brother Carl. "Come on, wake up!"
He shook her arm again. "Hurry up or you'll miss riding the train."

Alicia woke suddenly, her heart beating loudly in her chest. She felt like she couldn't breathe. The train ride! Everyone was excited about riding the train. Everyone except Alicia.

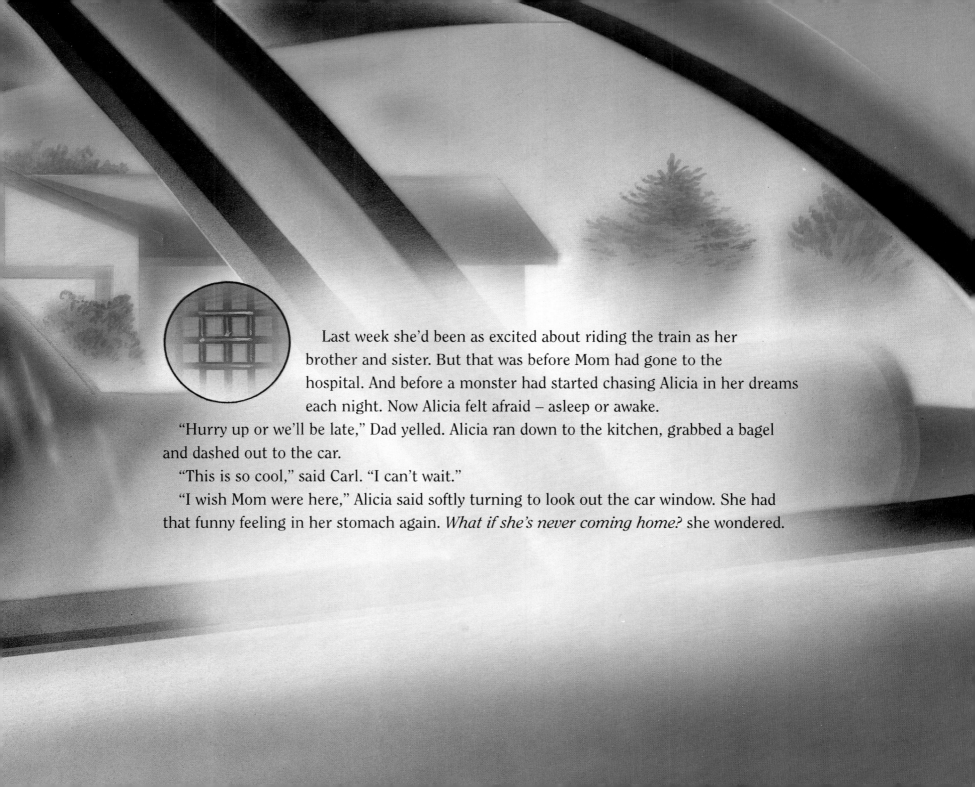

Last week she'd been as excited about riding the train as her brother and sister. But that was before Mom had gone to the hospital. And before a monster had started chasing Alicia in her dreams each night. Now Alicia felt afraid – asleep or awake.

"Hurry up or we'll be late," Dad yelled. Alicia ran down to the kitchen, grabbed a bagel and dashed out to the car.

"This is so cool," said Carl. "I can't wait."

"I wish Mom were here," Alicia said softly turning to look out the car window. She had that funny feeling in her stomach again. *What if she's never coming home?* she wondered.

The warmth of the car heater soon lulled Alicia to sleep. Her nightmare returned. The awful roaring noise filled the car. Alicia tried to run away but the creepy mist began closing in on her again. It wrapped itself around her leg. Panicky with fear, Alicia jerked free and began to run.

She found herself in a strange place. A beautiful white light sparkled in front of her. Something about the light made her feel safe, but when Alicia reached out to touch it, the light danced away.

The light seemed to slide down a rainbow and disappear through a door in a big oak tree. How could that be? Alicia ran to the tree and peeked inside.

Behind her she heard the clanking sound again. Alicia bolted inside and slammed the door shut to lock out the scary noise and the awful mist.

"Hello, Alicia," said a woman she didn't know. "I'm Mrs. Murgatroyd, and I'm so glad you came."

"How did you know my name?" asked Alicia.

"I know all the children who need my magical paints," said Mrs. Murgatroyd with a smile.

Alicia couldn't take her eyes off the rainbow. It was flowing into the paint pots — each color pouring into its own pot.

"The rainbow gives the paints their magic," Mrs. Murgatroyd said. "Would you like to paint something?"

Alicia nodded. Mrs. Murgatroyd handed her some paper and set pots of paint beside her. Before she knew it, Alicia had filled the paper with a picture of the terrible mist. Then a strange thing happened. The mist began to swirl and from the center came the red glow of the monster's eye!

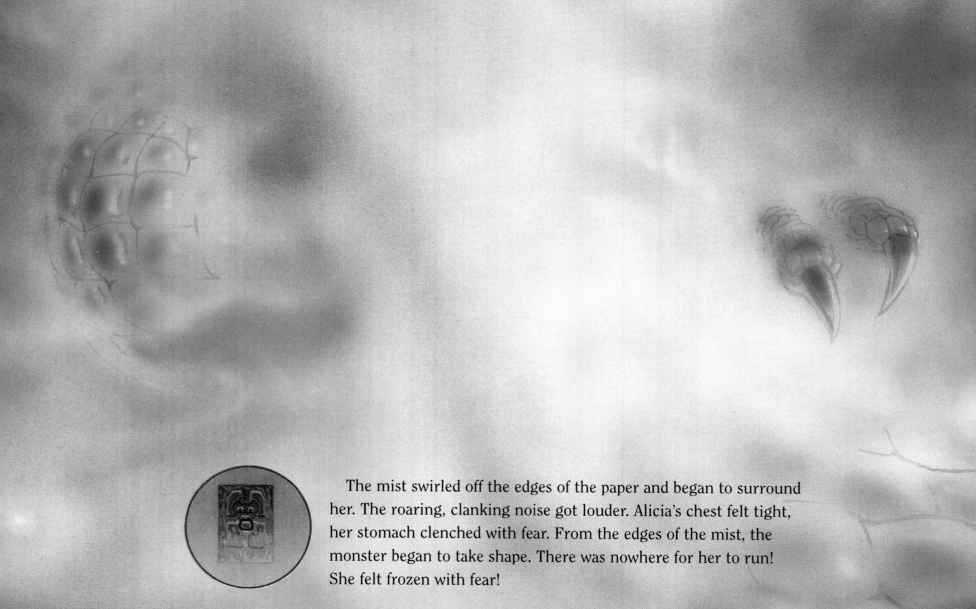

The mist swirled off the edges of the paper and began to surround her. The roaring, clanking noise got louder. Alicia's chest felt tight, her stomach clenched with fear. From the edges of the mist, the monster began to take shape. There was nowhere for her to run! She felt frozen with fear!

Suddenly the mist began to lift. Alicia could feel the hot breath of the monster blowing the mist past her. What was happening now? A long, low whistle pierced the air.

Wait a minute! Monsters can't whistle! Alicia peeked through her fingers. Sunlight was filtering through the thinning mist. Alicia's heart thudded loudly but she was excited, too.
She looked around her.

She was standing at the train station, and coming toward her was a huge steam engine. Jets of steam swirled across the silver tracks and smoke billowed from the smokestack. As the engine roared to a stop, the wheels screeched and clanked. *Is this the monster in my bad dreams?* she wondered.

Just then Alicia saw someone waving from a window. It was Mom! Alicia wanted to climb aboard the train, but she was still afraid. She didn't know what to do.

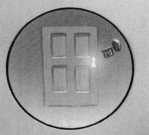

In her dream, her mother got off the train and Alicia ran to meet her. "I was afraid you'd never come home again," Alicia cried.

"It's okay to be afraid sometimes," said her mother as she gave Alicia a big hug. Just then jets of steam shot out from the wheels. Alicia pulled back in fright. With a loud clang, the engine began to huff and the whistle pierced the air.

"All aboard!" the conductor called.

Alicia felt afraid and excited at the same time as she took her mother's hand and climbed up the steps onto the train.
What will this be like? she wondered. This was the monster from the mist and she was climbing inside it! Alicia caught her breath as the train gave a jerk and began to pick up speed.

Towns and valleys looked like doll houses as they sped past. *This monster wasn't so scary after all!* Alicia thought with excitement.

Suddenly everything got dark, then so black Alicia couldn't even see her mother. They were in a long tunnel. The noises from the train bounced off the tunnel walls and seemed even louder than in her nightmares. Alicia's stomach knotted tightly.

Far away, a tiny white light sparkled. She relaxed and began to breathe again. "There's the end of the tunnel," she said out loud. It was fun watching the little dot of light get bigger and bigger as the train came out of the tunnel.

The scene in front of her took Alicia's breath away. She had never seen anything so beautiful! The snow-covered valley looked like a scene from a fairy tale. *I think I'll paint a picture of this when I get home,* Alicia thought happily.

A shrill whistle and a sudden jerk woke Alicia. There in front of the car was the train they had come to ride.

"It's about time you woke up," said her sister. "Hey, let's see if we can sit in the caboose!"

"I'm going to remember everything I see so I can tell Mom about it when she comes home," Carl said.

"That's a good idea," Dad said. "She'll be home in just a few days, and I know she'll want to hear all about this."

Rainbows of light seemed to dance across the shiny windows of the train. Alicia wasn't afraid at all. Far down the tracks the whistle blew and a conductor called, "All aboard!"

"Hurry up, Dad," Alicia called excitedly. "I don't want to miss the train ride!"